Date Due

Sunday for Sona

GLADYS YESSAYAN CRETAN

ILLUSTRATED BY BARBARA FLYNN

Lothrop, Lee & Shepard Company
NEW YORK

Other good books by
GLADYS YESSAYAN CRETAN
A Hole, a Box and a Stick
Messy Sally
Lobo
Lobo and Brewster
All Except Sammy
A Gift From the Bride
Because I Promised
Me, Myself and I

*U*p to now Sunday had always been Sona's favorite day. Every Sunday, when the doorbell rang, she ran and pulled the handle on the wall at the top of the stairs. This opened the door downstairs and one by one her San Francisco relatives came up.

"We come! We come!" called Uncle Levon.

"Here we are, Brother-in-law!" called Aunt Hrani, while Uncle Kosrove simply roared and laughed and laughed and roared.

Up they came, Sona's uncles and her great-uncles, her aunts and her cousins, as her father welcomed them one by one.

"What a noise!" Sona said. "There isn't a quiet Baronian in the family."

"And there isn't one who doesn't like to eat," her mother said, as they smelled the delicious food being carried up the stairs. The meat *beoregs*, the stuffed grape leaves, and the *manti* were still warm in their pans.

Nana smiled. "My family is my pleasure," she said.

The family gathered at Sona's house because Nana lived there, and Nana was now the oldest member of the family. Besides, Sona's house had the largest dining room, and this meant that everyone could sit for Sunday dinner together, with only a little squeezing.

Sometimes, if all the uncles and cousins came, and if too many happened to bring friends along, Sona and her cousins sat in the kitchen. David told riddles, and Johnny or Anna complained about school. It was fun, but it wasn't best, because no one wanted to miss a story by Uncle Kosrove.

In fact, Sona didn't want to miss any part of family Sunday. She liked being measured for having grown so much in only one week. She liked feeling herself watched with smiles as she passed the tray with tiny cups full of strong coffee in the living room after dinner.

"Soon she will be a lady," said Aunt Hrani.

"What of your school," asked Uncle Levon. "What do you study now?"

And always someone said, "I hope you have been practicing the piano." Because in the family it was understood that all well-brought-up Armenian girls should play an instrument—usually the piano, sometimes the violin. Once Sona had asked if she couldn't learn the clarinet instead, but Nana had quickly said, "To blow a horn? It is not ladylike." And that was the end of it.

Up to now, Sona hadn't minded when Nana wanted her to be a lady. It was fun to help with the baking. It was fun to have the table set and the

dinner ready when her mother and her father came from work. Sometimes even practicing the piano was fun, especially when she was close to learning a new piece to play for the family on Sunday.

But now she had something else she really wanted to do, something she thought about all the time—sailing.

And the only way to do it was to sneak out and run. Sneak—that was Nana's fault. Sona had tried to explain, but Nana said no. No sailing. And Sona knew that if Nana said no, that was that. Her parents would simply say she must not worry Nana.

Since the first time Sona had gone to the nearby harbor with her friend Tommy to look at his uncle's sailboat, she had hardly been able to think of anything but the slap of the water against the boats and the tangy smell of salt in the wind. There was the mystery of where that wind blew in from, and the feeling of real adventure. And she hadn't even been out on the bay yet. That was coming soon.

She owed it all to Tommy. As soon as his uncle mentioned that he had bought a boat, Tommy asked if Sona could come with him to see it. He dashed down the stairs of his flat and ran the long block to Sona's house.

"Come on!" he gasped. "A boat! A boat in my own family—and we can go on it!"

They hurried down the long stretch of blocks to

the Marina Green, and finally to the docks of the yacht harbor. They looked at each boat carefully. Sona had a different feeling about them now. She noticed the curve of the bow, the size of the cabins, the carving on a rail.

When they finally came to the *North Star*, with Uncle Jerry O'Brien hard at work, Sona pulled in her breath.

"It's beautiful," she said.

"Our own boat," Tommy said.

After that Sona and Tommy worked every afternoon. They helped with the sanding, the painting and varnishing. Uncle Jerry O'Brien finished rerigging the tall mast. The boat was seaworthy again. They could chug out of the harbor into the bay and then hoist their sails as they had watched so many others do. Sona and Tommy would become real sailors.

If only Nana had understood.

"You are repairing a boat?" Nana had said. "I don't know if that is ladylike."

"Oh, Nana," Sona said, "it's a beautiful boat. And Tommy's uncle is a real sailor. He's sailed all over the world."

"If you want to go and see the boat, fine," Nana said. "But why must you sand and paint?"

"Because," Sona said, "whoever helps repair the boat gets to go for the first sail. Mr. O'Brien bought

THE NORTH STAR

it from another man, and it needs lots and lots of paint and varnish. Then we're going to sail it right into the bay, Nana."

Nana was stunned.

"Into the bay?" She shook her head. "Your mother and father are trusting me to raise you safely, as well as to be a lady. The bay sounds dangerous. I must think. We will say nothing to the family until I have decided if it is yes or it is no."

Sona tried not to think about that "no."

Every day after school she and Tommy walked as fast as they could down the long city blocks, past the flats and apartments, down to the harbor. This much Nana would allow.

Through foggy days and sunny days they scraped and they sanded until their fingers ached, but they didn't mind. They would listen to Mr. O'Brien tell about the storms and the winds he had fought, and about the people he met in strange ports—sometimes as skipper of beautiful big yachts, sometimes on his own smaller boats.

"Someday I'm going to Tahiti," Tommy said.

"And I'm going to Bombay," said Sona.

"Why not?" said Tommy's uncle. "A sailor starts by dreaming."

When they began to paint the deck, Sona came home with dark stains on her fingers.

"What is that ugliness?" Nana said. "Will it wash off?"

"No," Sona said. "I've tried already. But it doesn't matter."

"Doesn't matter?" said Nana. "Of course it matters. If you want to continue with this foolishness you must at least wear gloves while you paint."

"Nana," said Sona, "sailors don't wear gloves."

"Sailors?" said Nana. "Who is thinking of sailors? I am thinking of ladies. Ladies do not have ugly stained hands."

The next day Sona tried wearing Nana's rubber gloves. It made her fingers feel thick, and before she knew it she had spilled a can of paint.

"Watch it!" called Mr. O'Brien.

Sona's face felt hot.

"I guess a real sailor would never do that," she said as she cleaned it up.

"Takes a long time to become a real sailor," said Jerry O'Brien. "It's not only a matter of deciding. You practice the piano every day. Couldn't just say 'I'm a piano player' and then be one."

"The trouble is," said Sona, "that it's hard to be a piano player and a sailor too."

"Music and sailing," said Jerry O'Brien. "Two of the best things in the world. Why give one up?"

I won't, Sona thought. Even if I have to run away to sea. But it was hard to picture running

away with a great big piano. And even harder to picture taking the whole family along. Sona wondered how she would ever work it out.

It wasn't easy, either, to practice the piano with fingers that were not only stained but scraped raw and blistered.

On Sunday, when she played for her aunts and uncles, they looked at each other and then back at her in surprise.

"Something is wrong?" asked Uncle Kosrove. "You have been ill and not practicing?"

"She's having an off day," said her mother. "That's all. Johnny, play your violin for us now."

"Sure," said Johnny, "but why doesn't Sona tell us what's the matter? And why do her hands look funny?"

"Never mind," said Nana. "Soon will be time to tell and then she'll tell."

Yes, Sona thought. Next Sunday. That was the day her two worlds would bump into each other. That was the day the boat would be ready to sail. They would hoist the sails and take a trial run right into San Francisco Bay. Mr. O'Brien, Tommy, and Sona. Captain, mate, and crew. That is, if the crew was there.

Johnny finished playing the violin and now Uncle Levon picked up his oud, strummed a few chords,

and started to sing. He sang a sad-beautiful song, and something in it made Sona feel she could tell Uncle Levon about the boat, about the bay, and about the sea that Jerry O'Brien had sailed and that she wanted to sail too. But she didn't, because Nana had said to say nothing till she decided.

Sona knew she couldn't wait much longer, because Mr. O'Brien had said she absolutely had to have her family's permission. Or better yet, one of them could come along. Otherwise she couldn't go on the maiden voyage of the fresh new *North Star*. What if she couldn't get Nana's permission?

Sona tried to ask on Monday. The words wouldn't come out.

She tried on Tuesday. Nothing happened.

On Thursday she closed her eyes and thought the words for the hundredth time, and she must have said her thoughts out loud, because she heard Nana answering, "No! No, I have decided against it. To sail into that great bay! In a tiny boat! Do you think we found you on the streets, to take such a chance with you?"

"It's not a chance," Sona said. "Mr. O'Brien has sailed clear around the world, and he's been training us. Especially Tommy. He's going to be first mate."

Nana kept rolling out some dough. She said nothing.

"Besides," Sona went on, "Mr. O'Brien knows

we both can swim, and by Sunday he'll buy some new life jackets."

Nana's rolling pin stopped.

"Sunday?" she exclaimed. "Did you say Sunday?"

"Mr. O'Brien said it would be after church," Sona said in a tiny voice.

"Certainly. After church," Nana said. "But what of dinner? What of the family?"

"We'll try not to be back too late," Sona said miserably. "You said you would really think about it."

"Yes," Nana said, "and I am a lady who keeps her word. I have been thinking about it. About sailing. Which is hard enough. And about meeting Mr. O'-Brien. But not about changing our whole family life. No. That is too much."

No. That was the answer.

After all the scraping and sanding and painting. No.

After all the dreams of sailing with the wind. No.

And those dreams of faraway, mysterious ports.

Just plain no.

On Sunday as Sona set the large dining-room table she could hear her mother and her grandmother bustling about in the kitchen. When she heard the noisy sizzling and gurgling of food cooking, and the clatter of baking tins pulled from the oven, she thought, "Now!" and ran quietly down the stairs. She ran past the apartments, past the houses, till finally, out of breath, she came to the docks. She really had run away to sea!

She stood at the pier to catch her breath, and watched the boats, large boats and small, rising and falling in the water. They looked so comfortable, so exactly right. Then why did she feel so exactly wrong?

Because I know I shouldn't be here, she thought.

But she knew she couldn't stay away either.

Down the docks she saw Mr. O'Brien and Tommy, arms full of the great bulky sails, starting to attach them to the mast.

Mr. O'Brien would feel sure she had permission to sail. He would never guess. . . . She decided not to think about it. She couldn't. It was too mixed up.

She ran toward the boat. "Here I am!" she called.

"Ah, the crew," said Jerry O'Brien. "Welcome aboard! Can you handle the jib?"

"Sure!" said Sona. She shook the jib sail out of its bag and clambered over the top of the cabin. She snapped the jib onto the tall forestay.

"Good work," Mr. O'Brien said. "You remembered everything. I hope someone from your family is coming."

"Well," Sona said, "well . . . "

"Sona!" Tommy called. "Is that your grandmother walking down the dock?"

"It can't be!" Sona said. She pulled her breath in.

It was.

There was Nana, in her black coat and her little black hat, scarf blowing in the wind. There walked Nana, her back straight and her step brisk. But somehow to Sona she looked small and alone.

"Say," Mr. O'Brien said, "it's good of her to come to see us off. I'll feel better, too, knowing her personally."

Sona didn't answer. She slid down into the cockpit and peered out. She wondered if there was a better place to hide. She couldn't face Nana.

"What's she carrying?" Tommy asked.

"That's her satchel," Sona said.

"What's in it?" Tommy asked.

"Sometimes treats," Sona said. "But I don't think she'll have treats today."

"Why not?" Jerry O'Brien said. "It's a special day."

Nana looked carefully at each boat she passed. She came nearer and nearer. It was getting too late for Sona to run.

But suddenly she did run. Straight to her grandmother.

"Oh, Nana," she said as she threw her arms around her, "I'm sorry. I shouldn't have run away!"

Nana looked down at Sona's face and nodded gently. She put her satchel down and gave Sona a hug. For a long moment neither one spoke.

"Never mind," Nana said finally. "I have been

wrong too. I know you have never deceived me before. So I had to think—what has driven you to it this time? I know, I left you with too hard a choice. And we did not talk about it enough. Now, never mind. I have come to see this *North Star*, and to meet the sailor, O'Brien."

"A pleasure, ma'am," called Jerry O'Brien. "I hope you'll sail with us."

"There is room?" Nana asked.

"Certainly," Jerry O'Brien said. "Sails four easily. Even five."

"Oh, Nana," Sona said, "You don't have to. Not for me. I don't think you'll like it."

Nana looked at her sternly. "I came to this country on a big ship," she said. "I sailed before you were born."

"Good for you," said Jerry O'Brien. "That settles it." He reached out and helped her onto the boat. "Welcome aboard," he said.

Nana opened her satchel and pulled out a brightly wrapped bottle.

"I thought we might have a christening ceremony," she said.

"You mean break the bottle?" said Sona. "On our fresh paint?"

"Maybe splinter the wood?" Tommy said.

"Perhaps we could drink a toast instead," said Mr. O'Brien.

"Exactly as I thought," said Nana. She handed each one a small paper cup. "We have grape juice," she said. "Sona's favorite drink."

"Ma'am," said Jerry O'Brien, "my hat's off to you. You've thought of everything. Tommy, get your harmonica. Can't have a celebration without music."

He lifted his cup. "Happy voyages, *North Star*," he said. They stood in place as Tommy played "Anchors Aweigh."

Nana smiled. "Good," she said. "A song of the sea."

Now Tommy started the motor and Mr. O'Brien took charge of the tiller, steering the boat past the row of small boats at the dock.

Nana and Sona sat opposite each other. "Beautiful," Nana nodded as they looked ahead at the opening sight of the bay.

"Wind's perfect," Mr. O'Brien said. "Man the tiller, Tommy, and I'll hoist the sails. Hold her into the wind."

In a moment the white sails rose. First the large mainsail, then the smaller sail, the jib. With the motor turned off now, the boat began to rock with the waves and the wind.

Sona caught her breath. After all this time it was really happening. "We're sailing!" she said. "We're really sailing."

"Look at that," Nana said. "Like wings."

"See, Nana," Sona said. "Over there is the Golden Gate. You go through there and on to the South Seas. Maybe to Tahiti."

"Wind's shifting," Mr. O'Brien said. "I'll take the tiller again. Sona, you're in charge of the jib. Now as I call, let the jib go. Ready about! Hard-a-lee!"

The small sail swung around to the other side of the boat.

"Tighten the jib sheet!" called Mr. O'Brien. "Pull!"

The ropes bit into Sona's hands. She pulled as hard as she could, and finally made them fast to a cleat on the deck.

Nana moved quickly from her seat to the one across.

"Balance the weight," she said.

"Mrs. Baronian," said Jerry O'Brien, "you are a natural sailor."

"Certainly," said Nana.

"Coming to a choppy patch of water," said Jerry O'Brien.

"Good," Nana said.

The boat rolled, tipped. It found its balance again.

"Good," she said again. "Now we are matching wits with the sea."

"Right," said Jerry O'Brien, as water came splashing over the rail.

Sona didn't think it was so good at all.

"It was better when it was smoother," she said.

"But this is more exciting," Tommy said.

Sona held onto a rail as the boat tipped and tilted. The waves were getting larger. The boat was leaning, leaning, almost into the water. A strange something inside her seemed to be going round and round in a wavy pattern. The spray on her face was salty. Too salty. She wondered why she had liked the smell of salt water. She didn't like it now. She didn't like being so wet. She didn't like anything.

Her eyes kept trying to close against the bright light. But she had to stay awake. She had to be in charge of the jib.

Now that thing inside of her was floating up and down. Up and down.

Suddenly the boat lurched.

"Tighten that jib!" called Jerry O'Brien. "Tighten it!"

But Sona's eyes felt heavy and her fingers felt mushy.

"Let me!" Nana said. She grasped the rope firmly.

"More!" said Jerry O'Brien. Then, "Good! Good for you, Mrs. Baronian."

"It is nothing," said Nana. "Just sense."

"We're almost out of it," Tommy said as the boat leveled itself. "I wasn't even scared. Were you, Sona?"

Sona didn't answer.

"We can bear off now," said Mr. O'Brien. "We're all right."

"Are we?" Sona said in a small voice. "We're still bobbing up and down."

"This is nothing," Mr. O'Brien said. "It's a beautiful breeze."

Nothing seemed beautiful to Sona. "It smells strange," she said.

"The smell of the seven seas," Nana said.

"Right," said Jerry O'Brien, "and we have a southwest wind. We can sail on this tack all the way to Sausalito."

"Is it far?" Sona asked.

"We'll go as far as we like," Mr. O'Brien said.

Sona thought she had already done that.

Nana dipped into her satchel again. "I brought *cheoregs*," she said. "Pastries, but not sweet."

"Lucky you thought of it," Tommy said. "I'm hungry."

"A treat," said Mr. O'Brien.

"Sona," said Nana. "Your *cheoreg*?"

But Sona didn't answer. She closed her eyes and wished the boat would stop rocking. She wondered how they could eat. Maybe she would never eat again.

"Sona!" Nana said again. "Don't you want a *cheoreg*?"

"No," Sona said, her eyes still closed. "Please, no."

"Ah," Nana said. "A feeling from the sea. I remember. Here, I have something better for you." She found a package of soda crackers. "Try."

Sona tried two. But it didn't help. Even her face felt stiff. And with each roll of the boat she felt worse. And worse.

Nana shook her head. "Too bad," she said.

Mr. O'Brien nodded. "It is too bad," he agreed. "But I'll tell you one thing, this is supposed to be a pleasure trip, and if it's not a pleasure for Sona we'll turn back. No sense in it."

Now Sona felt more miserable, because she was spoiling the sail for everyone else. But mostly she wanted to get home and lie down.

When the boat had been tied up, the first thing they did was to let Sona off. She sat on the dock, and was surprised at how quickly she felt better.

When the sails were down and in the sail bags, Nana shook hands with Mr. O'Brien.

"Thank you for taking me," she said. "It was adventure."

"My pleasure," said Mr. O'Brien. "In fact, I appreciated your help, since I lost part of my crew."

Sona's face grew hot.

"I'm sorry, Mr. O'Brien," she said. "I guess I'm not a sailor at all."

"Foolishness!" said Nana. "You will become one.

It is in your blood!"

"She's right," said Mr. O'Brien. "Lots of new sailors have trouble at first. You'll come around."

Maybe, Sona thought. Maybe.

Nana turned to Mr. O'Brien. "I hope you and Tommy will come home with us," she said. "Our whole family waits to have Sunday dinner."

"We wouldn't want to interfere in a family party," said Jerry O'Brien.

"Friends are family," Nana said. "Come!"

As they went up the stairs at home, there was a roar of welcoming noise.

"Here they are!" called Sona's mother. "The sailors!"

"Home from the sea!" roared Uncle Kosrove.

Sona threw her arms around her father. "I shouldn't have run away like that," she said.

"No," he said, "you really shouldn't have."

"And besides, I'm not even a good sailor. But Nana is."

"Child," said Nana, "I told you to stop worrying. You will sail proudly. You'll see."

"Your mother is a born sailor," Jerry O'Brien said to Sona's father.

"Hear! Hear!" roared Uncle Kosrove.

"Come, Mr. O'Brien," said Auntie Julia. "Come

sit here at the table and tell us of your travels. And Tommy, you sit by me."

This time everyone squeezed in at the large dining table, not to miss a word, because there were two storytellers. They heard tales of Madagascar, and tales of Samoa.

After dinner Sona passed the coffee in the living room.

Uncle Levon picked up his oud. "Now I will sing a song of the Armenian waters," he said. "But not of a sea. I sing of a lake."

Smoothly, smoothly, his voice soared and dipped. They saw the rippling waters and the moon.

Once again Sona felt that her Uncle Levon would understand whatever she might tell him. From now on, she would remember that.

"Now," Uncle Kosrove said, "now, Jerry O'Brien, let us hear you sing a song of the seas that you know."

Jerry O'Brien broke into a lilting chant from the South Sea Islands.

"Ah," said Uncle Kosrove when the song was finished. "Sona, you have brought us a fine friend. A fine friend."

"A treasure from the sea," said Nana.

"And now," said Aunt Julia, "let us hear the piano. Come, Sona."

Sona looked around the room at the pleased faces

of the family. She saw Uncle Levon nodding happily as she walked toward the piano.

Then she stopped.

"I have a better idea," she said. "Most of you didn't get to hear Tommy play for the christening of the *North Star*."

"She is right," Nana said. "We have not had this chance before. Tommy must play his harmonica."

"Of course," said the uncles. "Yes! Please," said the aunts.

Tommy's face looked pink behind freckles, but he pulled the harmonica out of his pocket.

Once again he started to play "Anchors Aweigh."

"I know that song," Cousin Johnny said.

"Then sing!" said Uncle Jerry O'Brien.

And Johnny did. The uncles did too. And then the aunts joined in, and Sona's mother and father.

"We sail at break of da-a-a-ay . . . " they all sang. All except Nana. She clapped to the beat, because she didn't know the words.

Sona looked around the circle, and thought there had never been a better Sunday. It was strange. All in one day, everything was different, and yet everything was still the same.

"Here's wish-ing you a hap-py voyage home!" she sang.